Quick Guide to Evaluating Information Online

Bradley Steffens

San Diego, CA

© 2025 ReferencePoint Press, Inc.
Printed in the United States

For more information, contact:
ReferencePoint Press, Inc.
PO Box 27779
San Diego, CA 92198
www.ReferencePointPress.com

ALL RIGHTS RESERVED.
No part of this work covered by the copyright hereon may be reproduced or used in any form or by any means—graphic, electronic, or mechanical, including photocopying, recording, taping, web distribution, or information storage retrieval systems—without the written permission of the publisher.

LIBRARY OF CONGRESS CATALOGING-IN-PUBLICATION DATA

Names: Steffens, Bradley, 1955- author.
Title: Quick guide to evaluating information online / by Bradley Steffens.
Description: San Diego, CA : ReferencePoint Press, Inc., [2025] | Includes bibliographical references and index.
Identifiers: LCCN 2024015309 (print) | LCCN 2024015310 (ebook) | ISBN 9781678208141 (library binding) | ISBN 9781678208158 (ebook)
Subjects: LCSH: Disinformation--Juvenile literature. | Information literacy--Juvenile literature.
Classification: LCC HM1231 .S845 2025 (print) | LCC HM1231 (ebook) | DDC 028.7--dc23/eng/20240430
LC record available at https://lccn.loc.gov/2024015309
LC ebook record available at https://lccn.loc.gov/2024015310

Introduction 4
Unfiltered Information

Chapter One 8
Identifying False and Misleading Information

Chapter Two 18
Spotting Deepfakes and Altered Images

Chapter Three 27
Recognizing Bias

Chapter Four 37
Eluding Online Scammers

Chapter Five 46
Avoiding Imposters

Source Notes	55
For Further Research	59
Index	61
Picture Credits	64
About the Author	64

INTRODUCTION

Unfiltered Information

On January 23, 2024, amid the war between Hamas and Israel, the Quds News Network, a Palestinian youth news agency, posted a disturbing video on X (formerly Twitter). The video showed an array of black tin cans. The off-screen narrator, speaking in Arabic, said that the cans were explosive devices disguised as cans of food. He stated, "In case anyone opens the can in the wrong way, it will immediately explode which might lead to the amputation or the death of the person who attempted to open the can."[1] The narrator turned the cans over to reveal the trigger mechanisms. In the post containing the video, Quds News Network stated, "According to local sources, Israeli jets dropped cans containing explosives as bait for starving displaced Palestinians in Al Mawasi in southern Gaza. Two children, one man, and one woman were killed by the fake cans."[2] By April 2024 the post had more than 2.1 million views.

The video and the accompanying text were a hoax, according to independent fact-checker Ryan McBeth. "These are not meat cans. They are the containers of M603 land mine fuses," writes McBeth. "The box the fuses were stored in is visible in the video. We may even have a partial lot number on the box." According to McBeth, the post is misinformation—false information presented as fact. "Bad actors count on the fact that you can't identify a land mine fuse in order to push their propaganda," writes McBeth. "Fight back with knowledge."[3]

Masses of Misinformation

Misinformation is not new, but the ability to distribute it to millions of people in a matter of days or even hours is, thanks to the internet and especially social media. Also, in the past only a limited number of people—those with access to a means of publishing or broadcasting—could spread misinformation. Today anyone with a smartphone can post a video, meme, or message on TikTok, Instagram, or Facebook, regardless of whether the content is accurate. There are no human gatekeepers to the world of online information, only software designed to flag the most offensive social media posts, usually those containing hate speech, violence, or pornography. A few software filters comb text postings for falsehoods, but those focus mostly on the words of elected officials and topics of extreme importance, such as medical misinformation.

The creators of the World Wide Web relished the idea that users would be free to share their thoughts and creations with the world. This dream has become a reality, and the diversity of expression has enriched humankind. People today know more about the goings on in every part of the world than ever before. But this freedom has also created problems. Large numbers of internet users post and repost information without bothering to check whether it is true. Companies selling products or organizations promoting causes flood social media with half-truths that lead consumers to false conclusions. People with malicious intent, often called bad actors, tell outright lies to enrich themselves or gain political power.

Many observers conclude that false information has a detrimental effect on society. The debate over social and political issues is complex because opposing sides not only have differing opinions but also disagree on the underlying facts that support and sustain those opinions. If people cannot agree on what problems they face, they will never agree on what solutions they should implement. Many argue that this fragmented worldview

Thanks to the internet and especially social media, misinformation can now be distributed to millions of people in a matter of days or even hours.

makes consensus impossible, leaving only splintered, warring factions. "On page one of any political science textbook it will say that democracy relies on people being informed about the issues so they can have a debate and make a decision," says Stephan Lewandowsky, a cognitive scientist at the University of Bristol in the United Kingdom. "Having a large number of people in a society who are misinformed and have their own set of facts is absolutely devastating and extremely difficult to cope with."[4]

Confronting the Lies

Some experts believe that artificial intelligence (AI)—like the kind used to moderate posts on Instagram, Facebook, and X—can promote reasoned debate by labeling and even banning false information. "AI can be a powerful tool to improve content moderation and detect fake news on social media,"[5] states a report issued by the European Union in October 2023. Others think that using AI to moderate content is a bad idea. AI has trouble understanding nuanced speech and might mistake satire for serious misinformation. AI also trains itself on what it culls from the internet, so majority opinions might rise to the top while minority views get silenced.

> "AI can be a powerful tool to improve content moderation and detect fake news on social media."[5]
>
> —European Union

Beyond what social media platforms may do to reduce misinformation, most analysts argue that individual internet users need to become savvier about what they consume. Misinformation and outright lies can lead people to fall for scams that might result in a loss of time, money, or personal data. They need to be aware of the dangers of false information and be more skeptical of what they see and read. These critics maintain that the public must use critical thinking to analyze information before they accept it as true and then end up being swindled or unwittingly spreading falsehoods.

CHAPTER ONE

Identifying False and Misleading Information

On January 26, 2023, Jamie, an Instagram user known as Unapologetic Patriot Mama, posted a video on Instagram that featured Carlos Reyes, the host of *The Splendid Savage Podcast*, speaking about the war in Ukraine. Reyes gave a recap of the money the United States had provided to Ukraine after Russia invaded that nation in early 2022. Reyes said that the United States had sent $91.3 billion to Ukraine in nine months. Totals for the aid to Ukraine vary, but the number was roughly correct. However, Reyes said that the amount sent to Ukraine was double the US expenditure for its own war in Afghanistan. This was false. A report from the Special Inspector General for Afghanistan Reconstruction says the United States spent $849.7 billion in Afghanistan. That is almost ten times the amount spent in Ukraine at the time of the video. Unapologetic Patriot Mama's post is a classic example of online misinformation—in this case a mixture of facts and lies combined to confuse the public about how much the support of Ukraine was costing taxpayers.

The internet is awash in misinformation. According to the consumer data company Statista, 67 percent of Americans have encountered misinformation on social media, and 10 percent of

US adults have knowingly shared misinformation. "It's a huge problem, it's one of the biggest problems that we're dealing with right now," says Min-Seok Pang, an associate professor of management information systems and the Milton F. Stauffer Research Fellow at Temple University. "Fake news is becoming a 'life-and-death' matter and eroding trust and respect with each other, which is a backbone of any civilized society."[6]

> "Fake news is becoming a 'life-and-death' matter and eroding trust and respect with each other, which is a backbone of any civilized society."[6]
>
> —Min-Seok Pang, associate professor of management information systems at Temple University

Suspicious Motives

One reason for the vast amount of misinformation is that there is no single source or cause for its creation. Internet users post false information for a variety of reasons. Some, like Unapologetic Patriot Mama, have a political agenda. Others are unhappy workers who want to harm the reputation of their employer or former employer. Still others are in business, and they want to profit from misleading statements. Some make false statements to win elections and gain power.

Public officials and political candidates are seldom punished for their lies. They cannot be sued for making false statements unless they know the statements are false when they make them. In addition, the false statement must harm another person. This harm must be financial or able to be measured in some other way. The requirements for suing a public figure were established in a Supreme Court case known as *New York Times Co. v. Sullivan* (1964). In this decision, the court explained that even false speech must be protected if it is part of the political discourse. "Erroneous statement is inevitable in free debate," wrote Justice William Brennan for the majority. "It must be protected if the freedoms of expression are to have the 'breathing space' that they 'need . . . to survive.'"[7]

9

Free from meaningful penalties, politicians can spread false messages at will. They can do this by themselves, with the help of their supporters, or with the use of software programs known as bots, short for *robots*. Bots can automatically post thousands of messages in seconds, overwhelming the public with misinformation. Political campaigns do not always spread their lies to change voters' opinions. Sometimes, they simply want to create doubt in the voters' minds. A voter who is confused or turned off by false information might not vote at all, which helps the campaign that has targeted supporters of the opposition with negative messages.

The spread of political misinformation does not bode well for the future of democracy, according to Merten Reglitz, associate professor of philosophy at the University of Birmingham in the United Kingdom. "Major democratic institutions . . . have correctly identified fake news as a threat to their values and processes, but the real danger lurks in the corrosive effect that these online lies have on citizens' trust in their democracy," says Reglitz. "Fake

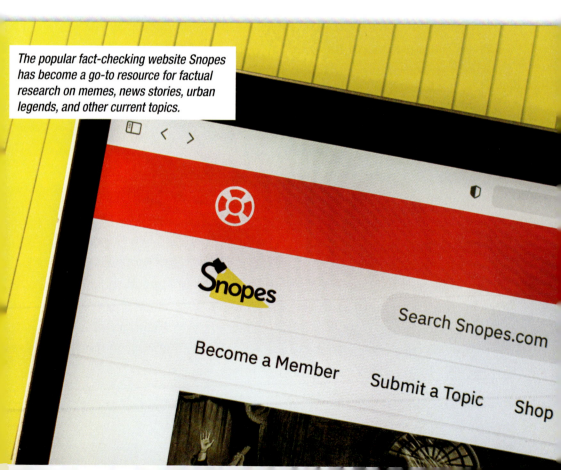

The popular fact-checking website Snopes has become a go-to resource for factual research on memes, news stories, urban legends, and other current topics.

news leads to a loss of trust of citizens in each other—a major cause of destabilising democratic processes and undermining the benefits that morally justify democratic institutions."[8]

Countering Misinformation

From its inception, the internet has been a breeding ground for false information. Conspiracy theories, urban legends, and political deception all found a home on the unregulated frontier of the internet. It did not take long for truth seekers to realize that something needed to be done to stem the rising tide of false information.

In 1994 David and Barbara Mikkelson founded a website called Urban Legends Reference Pages. As the name suggests, the website fact-checked urban legends, rumors, hoaxes, and folklore. Later, the Mikkelsons changed the name of the website to Snopes and expanded its fact-checking into a wider range of topics in American popular culture.

The success of Snopes inspired individuals and news organizations to launch similar websites, specializing in different things. Some of the best-known fact-checking websites include PolitiFact, AP Fact Check, and FactCheck.org. These organizations provide readers and news researchers with a means to determine the accuracy and truthfulness of claims, imagery, or audio circulating on the internet. PolitiFact mainly reports on statements by elected officials, political organizations, and candidates, but it also fact-checks cultural issues. It is one of several companies that has partnered with Meta, the corporation that owns Facebook and Instagram, to help identify false news and misinformation on its social networks' news feeds.

> "Major democratic institutions . . . have correctly identified fake news as a threat to their values and processes, but the real danger lurks in the corrosive effect that these online lies have on citizens' trust in their democracy."[8]
>
> —Merten Reglitz, associate professor of philosophy at the University of Birmingham

FactCheck.org reports mainly on political content—statements by politicians, social media posts attacking or defending elected officials, and claims about public policy. For example, the website reported on a viral video that showed army cadets rhythmically cheering at the annual army-navy football game on December 9, 2023. The cadets in the video could be heard chanting an offensive anti–President Joe Biden phrase. Experts at FactCheck.org analyzed the video and found that it had been altered. The cadets were not saying anything about Biden. The video was a hoax.

Policing Social Media

The growth of social media has caused a surge in online misinformation. This is because social media users were—and to some extent still are—free to post anything they like. They do not have to submit their posts to editors or fact-checkers prior to publication, the way writers for traditional media outlets do. The lack of editorial review means that social media users can spread information without regard to its truth.

As misinformation has spread through social media, critics commonly accuse the owners of the social networking platforms of not doing enough to counter the problem. Under pressure from watchdog groups, social media companies have begun to flag and even remove misinformation. This was not something the staffs at these companies could do by themselves, because the volume of social media posts is enormous. As a result, the social media companies have devised computer programs to monitor the content. Facebook pioneered this approach using an artificial intelligence program known as Deep Text. This program can analyze thousands of posts and comments every second. Instagram also uses Deep Text to moderate content. Google, which owns YouTube, devised its own AI systems to monitor the estimated 3.7 million new videos that are uploaded to YouTube every day.

Automated systems can be highly efficient. According to Statista, YouTube removed approximately 8.1 million videos in the third quarter of 2023 alone. The majority of these videos were quickly

Teens Susceptible to Fake Health News

According to a September 2022 study published in the scientific journal *Frontiers in Psychology*, many teenagers struggle with identifying fake health news. Researchers showed three hundred students aged sixteen to nineteen messages about the health benefits of fruits and vegetables. Half of the messages were true, and the other half were false. Researchers asked the students to judge the trustworthiness of each message. Forty-eight percent of the students found the truthful statements to be more trustworthy, but nearly as many—41 percent—found both statements to be equally trustworthy. Eleven percent found the fake messages more trustworthy than the true ones.

"As adolescents are frequent users of the internet, we usually expect that they already know how to approach and appraise online information, but the opposite seems to be true," says principal researcher Radomír Masaryk of Comenius University in Bratislava, Slovakia. Masaryk believes that teens need to develop analytical thinking and scientific reasoning "that help distinguish false from true health messages."

Quoted in Dennis Thompson, "Many Teens Easily Fooled by Fake Online Health Messages," Health-Day, September 2, 2022. www.healthday.com.

flagged by the company's automated system. Discussing the videos that YouTube removed in 2020, YouTube's chief product officer, Neal Mohan, said, "Over 50 percent of those videos were removed without a single view by an actual YouTube user, and over 80 percent were removed with less than 10 views. . . . That's the power of machines."[9]

Meta reports similar success in countering misinformation. In May 2022 Meta reported that from the beginning of the COVID-19 pandemic to June 2021, the company had displayed warnings on more than 190 million pieces of content that its fact-checking system rated as false, partly false, altered, or missing content. Meta also took action against bots and fake accounts that artificially boost engagement with misinformation. The company reported that from October to December 2021, its AI software detected and removed 1.7 billion fake accounts, often within minutes of registration.

Free Speech Concerns

While targeting misinformation on social media platforms has merits, it raises concerns about potentially suppressing freedom of speech. The First Amendment to the US Constitution prevents the government from restricting speech in a public forum, but private media companies generally are not required to follow that rule. They can set limits on the speech that they publish or broadcast. However, the government cannot force companies to limit what can or cannot be said or shown on their private platforms, even in the name of stopping misinformation. This became an issue in 2023, when the attorneys general of Missouri and Louisiana sued officials in the federal government to prevent them from pressuring social media companies into silencing viewpoints that questioned COVID-19 protocols and the validity of the 2020 presidential election.

On July 4, 2023, District Court judge Terry Doughty issued a preliminary injunction that barred several federal departments and agencies from "threatening, pressuring, or coercing social-media companies in any manner to remove, delete, suppress, or reduce posted content of postings containing protected free speech."[10] Doughty based his ruling on a Supreme Court case known as *Bantam Books, Inc. v. Sullivan* (1963). In that case the Rhode Island state legislature created a commission that notified private book distributing companies that certain publications were unfit for sale or display to minors and that booksellers could be arrested for selling books on the list. As a result, Rhode Island's largest book distributor stopped filling orders for books and magazines on the commission's list. The Supreme Court maintained that the state's law could not contravene the Constitution and that the commission had violated the First Amendment by pressuring the book distributors. "Their operation was in fact a scheme of state censorship effectuated by extra-legal sanctions; they acted as an agency not to advise but to suppress,"[11] Justice William Brennan wrote for the majority.

The federal government appealed Doughty's ruling to the Fifth Circuit Court of Appeals. The government argued that its agents were only giving the social media companies advice to combat dangerous misinformation. The Fifth Circuit Court of Appeals disagreed. It found that the thousands of documents presented to

14

Facebook's parent company, Meta, has taken action against bots and fake accounts that artificially boost engagement with misinformation.

Doughty showed the kind of conduct prohibited by *Bantam Books, Inc. v. Sullivan*. "The officials have engaged in a broad pressure campaign designed to coerce social-media companies into suppressing speakers, viewpoints, and content disfavored by the government," the court's three-judge panel wrote. "The harms that radiate from such conduct extend far beyond just the Plaintiffs; it impacts every social-media user."[12]

The court heard the Louisiana and Missouri cases together and ruled on them jointly. The government appealed the court's decision to the Supreme Court. The high court heard arguments on the case, known as *Murthy v. Missouri*, on March 18, 2024. Justice Samuel Alito questioned the federal government's appeal that it was not overreaching its authority by making requests of social media companies. "Both the district court found that the injury was traceable to the government's actions, and the Fifth Circuit accepted that finding," said Alito. "We don't usually reverse

Seeking Rewards, Not the Truth

According to researchers at Yale University and the University of Southern California, some social media users share misleading posts because the social media platforms reward them for doing so. "It's not that people are lazy or don't want to know the truth," says Gizem Ceylan, a researcher at the Yale School of Management. "The platforms' reward systems are wrong." In a paper published in *Proceedings of the National Academy of Sciences*, Ceylan's research team found that 15 percent of Facebook users—the 15 percent who use Facebook most often—were responsible for 37 percent of the false headlines. According to the study, these news sharers were not motivated by political beliefs:

> What we showed is that, if people are habitual sharers, they'll share any type of information, because they don't care [about the content]. All they care about is likes and attention. . . . It's a system issue, not an individual issue. We need to create better environments on social media platforms to help people make better decisions. We cannot keep on blaming users for showing political biases or being lazy for the misinformation problem. We have to change the reward structure on these platforms.

Quoted in Yale Insights, "How Social Media Rewards Misinformation," March 31, 2023. https://insights.som.yale.edu.

---

findings of fact that have been endorsed by two lower courts."[13] However, other justices were skeptical of the Fifth Circuit Court of Appeals ruling. They said that it is normal for the government to lobby private companies to take certain actions. They wondered whether the lower court's ruling was too broad and would prevent legitimate contact between the government and the social media companies. The Supreme Court's decision was due in June 2024.

The Role of Information Consumers

Whether content moderation is limited by the courts or not, some experts doubt that even the most advanced AI systems can solve the misinformation problem. "Many excellent methods will be developed to improve the information environment, but the history of online systems shows that bad actors can and will always find ways around them,"[14] says Paul N. Edwards, Perry Fellow in International Security at Stanford University. Faced with the prospect that misinformation will remain in circulation, it is up to internet users themselves to be part of the solution. "As a collective public, we all have the responsibility to stop the spread of disinformation,"[15] states the National Center for State Courts.

Lindsay Boezi, a reference assistant at the MacPhaidin Library, part of Stonehill College in Easton, Massachusetts, believes that internet users need to employ their critical-thinking skills when engaging with online information. "Think before you share," says Boezi. "Read the entire piece, not just the headline."[16] Emilio Ferrara, an associate professor at USC Annenberg, recommends doing a little research when encountering a story that sounds unlikely. He says:

> Before sharing something on Twitter or Facebook, it's crucial to assess the provenance, credibility and authority of the source of that news or information. Who published it? A well-established and credible person, or a shady account that maybe appears to post a lot of sensationalistic or divisive content? If there is a link in the post, where does the link point to? Is it a well-known news outlet or a maybe suspicious website?[17]

One person cannot end misinformation, but everyone has a role to play in combating it, says the Fraser Hall Library at the State University of New York College at Geneseo. "While you cannot stop this [false information] loop, you can avoid becoming part of it," states the library's website. "Always take a moment to fact check anything sensational before you repost."[18]

"As a collective public, we all have the responsibility to stop the spread of disinformation."[15]

—National Center for State Courts

CHAPTER TWO

Spotting Deepfakes and Altered Images

Billionaire pop star Taylor Swift is known for her generosity to friends, family, and staff. That is one reason why some of her fans believed a video in which the "Anti-Hero" singer seemed to offer a Le Creuset kitchenware giveaway in January 2024. "Hey y'all, it's Taylor Swift here," her image appeared to say. "Due to a packaging error, we can't sell 3,000 Le Creuset cookware sets. So I'm giving them away to my loyal fans for free."[19] Unfortunately for her fans, the offer was fake. Those who ordered were scammed out money to pay for shipping the nonexistent product. But Swift was not to blame. The speaker in the video looked and sounded like her, but it was not Swift. It was a deepfake—a realistic simulation of Swift's appearance and voice manufactured by artificial intelligence.

Machines Imitating Humans

Artificial intelligence refers to computer programming that can mirror some processes of human learning, such as reasoning and problem solving. Deepfakes take their name from the fact that they use AI's deep learning technology to create realistic video and audio recordings. Deep learning technology is a type of machine learning that recognizes and re-creates what a certain face looks like from different angles so it can be placed onto a target image as if it were a mask. The result is video that looks as if a familiar figure is saying or doing something that he or she did not say or do in real life. Using online websites to process the video files, almost anyone can create deepfake videos. According to independent researcher Genevieve Oh, more than 143,000 new deepfake videos were posted online in 2023.

Deepfakes, also known as synthetic media, have been used in the entertainment industry to create the illusion that a character has come back to life or that an actor from an earlier period is in a current film or program. For example, the creators of the 2023 American action-adventure film *Indiana Jones and the Dial of Destiny* had deep learning software scan footage of actor Harrison Ford from the early part of his career to create a lifelike simulation of the actor from all angles. They applied the deepfake technology to Ford's performance in the movie to "de-age" the actor by forty years.

Deepfakes are realistic simulations of a person's appearance and voice, manufactured by artificial intelligence. Taylor Swift is one of many celebrities whose appearance has been hijacked in deepfake scams.

Deepfakes are also used in advertising to capture viewer attention to sell a product. For example, a London-based company called Synthesia scans and analyzes the faces of paid actors to create digital likenesses, or avatars, that can be used to deliver any message in sixty-four languages. The company recently used its deepfake technology to revamp a commercial starring rapper and actor Snoop Dogg. The well-known performer appeared in a lavish TV commercial for the European food delivery service Just Eat. The company has a subsidiary in Australia named Menulog. Rather than hiring Snoop Dogg to reshoot the scenes in which he says the service's name, the company hired Synthesia to create a deepfake of the rapper saying "Menulog" instead of "Just Eat" in the commercial. "All of a sudden they had a localized version for the Australian market without Snoop Dogg having to do anything,"[20] says Synthesia cofounder and chief operating officer Victor Riparbelli.

Taking Disinformation to a New Level

The ability to create fake videos that are difficult to distinguish from real ones has raised concerns among law enforcement officials, security experts, and the military. In 2021 the Federal Bureau of Investigation (FBI) warned that Russian and Chinese propagandists were creating deepfake videos to spread anti-American messages on social media. "It is without a doubt one of the most important revolutions in the future of human communication and perception," says Nina Schick, author of *Deepfakes: The Coming Infocalypse*. "AI can now be used to make images and videos that are fake but look hyper realistic. From a disinformation perspective, this is a game changer."[21]

Deepfake technology has already been used as a propaganda weapon. In 2022, during the Russia-Ukraine war,

> "AI can now be used to make images and videos that are fake but look hyper realistic. From a disinformation perspective, this is a game changer."[21]
>
> —Nina Schick, author of *Deepfakes: The Coming Infocalypse*

A 2022 deepfake video of Ukrainian president Volodymyr Zelenskyy instructed Ukrainian citizens to lay down their arms and surrender to Russian invaders, sowing confusion among the public.

a video appeared on the website of the Ukrainian television station Ukrayina 24 that showed Ukrainian president Volodymyr Zelenskyy giving a speech. Standing behind a lectern, Zelenskyy appeared to tell Ukrainians to lay down their arms and surrender to the Russian invaders. The video was a deepfake. Russian hackers broke into the website of Ukrayina 24 and planted the phony video. It was then shared on local social media platforms Telegram and VK. The bogus video was instantly shared on larger platforms, including Facebook, Instagram, and Twitter. Zelenskyy denounced the video as fake on his official Instagram account, and the social media platforms soon removed it. "Neither well made nor believable, the Zelenskyy deepfake is among the worst I've seen," says BBC analyst Shayan Sardarizadeh. "But the fact a deepfake has now been made and shared during a war is notable. The next one may not be as bad."[22]

Government officials are concerned that more believable deepfakes might be used in the future. At a hearing before the US Senate

Select Committee on Intelligence, Nebraska senator Ben Sasse asked Director of National Intelligence Daniel R. Coats, "When you think about the catastrophic potential to public trust and to markets that could come from deep fake attacks, are we . . . organized in a way that we could possibly respond fast enough to a catastrophic deepfake attack?"[23] Coats replied, "We certainly recognize the threat of emerging technologies and the speed at which that threat increases. We clearly need to be more agile. We need to partner with our private sector."[24]

> "We certainly recognize the threat of emerging technologies and the speed at which that threat increases. We clearly need to be more agile. We need to partner with our private sector."[24]
>
> —Daniel R. Coats, director of national intelligence

Fighting AI with AI

Technology companies are rolling out possible solutions to the deepfake problem. Technology designer and manufacturer Intel has created an AI product called FakeCatcher. The company claims that FakeCatcher can analyze videos in milliseconds and detect fake videos with a 96 percent accuracy rate. One of the ways FakeCatcher does this is by looking for signs of blood flow in the pixels of a video. When human hearts pump blood, the veins under the skin subtly change color. FakeCatcher collects these blood flow signals from all over the face in the video. The machine's algorithms translate these signals into digital maps. FakeCatcher then compares the maps generated by the video to maps of real human blood flow. "Using deep learning, we can instantly detect whether a video is real or fake,"[25] says Ilke Demir, senior staff research scientist at Intel.

The vast majority of deepfakes are not of world leaders. Most are imitations of everyday people, whose images and voices are used to scam their friends and family members out of money. According to the Federal Trade Commission, Americans paid $1.6 billion to scammers in 2022. Many of these scams involved audio

Using AI to Improve Deepfakes

One technique deepfake creators use to make their images more realistic is a process known as generative adversarial networks. This process involves having two separate AI networks face off against each other as adversaries. One AI network generates an image, such as a human face. The other AI network then analyzes the image using machine learning, comparing the face to a database of other, real faces. It probes the image, looking for flaws, and when it has identified some, it generates an improved version of the image. The other AI network then takes its turn, analyzing the new face and trying to improve it. As the adversaries battle back and forth, the image becomes more and more convincing. The astonishing results of these battles are on display at a website called ThisPersonDoesNotExist.com. The images depict the faces of average-looking people. The viewer can see virtually every hair on the person's head and every facial pore. But it is all just an illusion. The images are of people who have never existed and never will. The faces are nothing more than the creations of the battling AI networks—flights of AI fancy rendered in photorealistic detail.

deepfakes, not video deepfakes. Scammers use AI technology to mimic the voices of an individual. They then call friends or family of the individual and use the deepfake voice to ask for money. "Any consumer, no matter their age, gender, or background, can fall victim to these ultra-convincing scams, and the stories we heard today from individuals across the country are heartbreaking," said Senator Bob Casey Jr. of Pennsylvania at a 2023 Senate hearing on deepfake scams. "As a parent and grandparent, I relate to the fear and concern these victims must feel."[26]

To create a sense of urgency, scammers make deepfake calls sound like the victim's loved one is in danger, injured, or being held hostage. One victim who testified at the Senate hearing, Terry Holtzapple, described how he and his wife were terrified by a deepfake call from what they believed was their daughter, LeAnn. "My daughter was, she was crying on the phone, profusely crying and

> "Any consumer, no matter their age, gender, or background, can fall victim to these ultra-convincing [deepfake] scams, and the stories we heard today from individuals across the country are heartbreaking."[26]
>
> —Bob Casey Jr., senator from Pennsylvania

Morgan Freeman Deepfake

To illustrate the power of synthetic media, Dutch filmmaker Bob de Jong created a deepfake video featuring the likeness of actor Morgan Freeman. Freeman himself had nothing to do with the video. De Jong had voice-over actor Boet Schouwink, known for his ability to imitate Freeman's voice, perform the script. De Jong replaced Schouwink's head and neck with an AI-generated digital mask that looks remarkably like Freeman. Since its release, the video has been viewed more than 13 million times on YouTube, TikTok, and X. The faux Freeman looks at the camera and delivers a cautionary message about deepfakes:

I am not Morgan Freeman, and what you see is not real—well, at least in contemporary terms it is not. What if I were to tell you that I am not even a human being. Would you believe me? What is your perception of reality? Is it the ability to capture, process and make sense of the information our senses receive?

If you can see, hear, taste or smell something, does that make it real? Or is it simply the ability to feel? I would like to welcome you to the era of synthetic reality. Now, what do you see?

Quoted in Diep Nep, *This Is Not Morgan Freeman—a Deepfake Singularity*, YouTube, July 7, 2021. https://youtu.be/oxXpB9pSETo?si=40zo25okapqRLqep.

saying, 'mom, mom, mom,' and of course my wife was saying, 'LeAnn, LeAnn, what is the matter?', and she repeated it again, 'mom, mom, mom' and it sounded exactly like her."[27]

The emotional nature of such calls can cloud the judgment of the person receiving the deepfake call. That is all part of the scammers' strategy, says Tahir Ekin, director of the Texas State Center for Analytics and Data Science. He told Casey's Senate committee that hearing the fear and stress in a loved one's voice increases the call's believability and emotional appeal. One of the problems with deepfakes is that many people—especially older people—are not aware that this technology has made its way out of the Hollywood studios and

"Prioritizing the enhancement of data and AI literacy among older Americans, and actively involving them in prevention and detection efforts, stands as a cornerstone [to preventing deepfake fraud]."[28]

—Tahir Ekin, director of the Texas State Center for Analytics and Data Science into the hands of online scammers. "Prioritizing the enhancement of data and AI literacy among older Americans, and actively involving them in prevention and detection efforts, stands as a cornerstone"[28] to preventing deepfake fraud, Ekin says.

Unmasking the Fakes

The Cybersecurity & Infrastructure Security Agency offers steps people can take to identify a deepfake. Viewers can look for physical features of images that defy reason, such as feet not touching the ground. Watchers can also examine shadows, reflections, and vanishing points to see whether they are consistent from one part of an image to another. For example, the location of shadows on one person might not align with the shadows on other people or objects. The shadows under a person's chin, nose, or arms might lie at slightly different angles than similar shadows on others. This is a sign that two images have been combined and the image is not genuine.

Users should also listen carefully to voices and noises on an audio track, whether part of a video or not. The audio may have

Calls from strangers that feature background noise, echo effects, or other confusing elements are cause for suspicion.

background noise added to help cover up any deficiencies in the voice simulation. Other audio effects, such as echo effects, might be a sign that audio filters are being used.

An internet user does not have to have expensive tools to investigate images. Browsers such as Bing and Google Chrome have built-in tools to conduct reverse image searches. These searches will show whether a photo has appeared elsewhere on the internet. For example, right-clicking on an image in Chrome will open a menu that includes the option "Search image with Google." Right-clicking an image in Bing will open a menu with the option "Search the web for image." Such searches may find other appearances of the same image and verify their authenticity. In some cases the photos that turn up may not include things that are in the photo being investigated. This will show that the image has been doctored in some way and cannot be trusted. The alternate images may also have captions with names and dates that are different from the image being investigated. Such inconsistencies may cast doubt on the reality of the image or at least challenge the context in which is being used.

Deepfakes may not be in their infancy, but they are still developing. It likely will not be long before deepfakes are undetectable to the naked eye. Even then, however, there are steps that internet users can take to defend themselves from deepfake fraud. Awareness is half the battle when combating deepfakes. Users must be aware that technology is making fakery more real and more difficult to detect than ever. When messages come from world leaders, politicians, or even entertainers, consumers should evaluate whether the views align with positions these personalities have endorsed in the past. Would they logically stake their reputation on the questionable message they seem to be supporting? As in other cases of suspected fraud, users can try to verify the truthfulness of any message by doing online research. If the deepfake involves a well-known person, chances are that one of the fact-checking organizations has already identified the deepfake, and this information is just a query away.

CHAPTER THREE

Recognizing Bias

People are inundated every day with torrents of information. This has always been true, but thanks to the internet, contemporary society is exposed to more information through more sources than ever before. There are not enough hours in a day for individuals to properly assess the information they encounter. As a result, people develop mental shortcuts to cope with information in their environment.

Cognitive Bias

One of the most effective—if limiting—of these coping mechanisms is known as cognitive bias. Rather than evaluating each piece of information in depth, individuals will either accept the information or dismiss it based on personal and sometimes unreasoned judgments—their cognitive bias.

Many cognitive biases are irrational. For example, people might avoid another person who looks a certain way because they once had a bad experience with someone who looked that way. They might prejudge a person based on appearance when they really know nothing about the person. It does not make sense, but people do it because they think it will protect them. Often, people are not even aware that they are engaging in this kind of bias. This is known as unconscious bias.

Other biases are more conscious. For example, people often develop political views based on their understanding of history and current affairs. In the United States people tend to look at the government in one of two ways: it either exists to protect the individual's rights or it is meant to further the good of society, even if doing so sometimes infringes on personal freedom. In the case of gun laws, those who believe the government exists to ensure individual liberty will likely see a fundamental right in the ability of a person to own a gun and even carry it in public. Those who believe the government is designed to better society will likely believe that it is acceptable to limit gun ownership and regulate it in a way that reduces gun violence. Once people have chosen sides in the debate, they are likely to develop a bias toward information about the issue. They do not reevaluate the issue each time it comes up. Instead, they apply their bias and move on.

Confirmation Bias

When encountering information, cognitive biases often arise in response to people's entrenched beliefs and their inability to process and examine everything they hear or see. Anchoring bias, for example, is the tendency to weigh more favorably a piece of information that is heard or viewed first and then compare all subsequent information against it. Confirmation bias is the

The then vice president Joe Biden addresses the audience at the Presidential Rally on Gun Safety in Des Moines, Iowa, on August 8, 2019. An event like this is popular with supporters but may fall on deaf ears among detractors.

practice of seeking out information that confirms a person's existing beliefs. It is another time-saving habit that helps people cope with vast amounts of information. The problem with confirmation bias is that it prevents people from hearing about or considering other points of view. Instead, they watch videos and read things that support their existing views. Anchoring bias and confirmation bias allow people to filter out, ignore, or reject information that conflicts with what they already accept as true. These biases limit how individuals interpret new information or differing viewpoints.

> "An echo chamber is a closed system where other voices are excluded by omission, causing your beliefs to become amplified or reinforced. In turn, these bubbles can boost social polarization and extreme political views."[29]
>
> —*Scientific Reports*, research published in 2024

News organizations, political parties, and other interest groups are aware of anchoring bias and confirmation bias. To attract an audience, these groups will often publish information that conforms to a bias. Such sources of information are sometimes known as echo chambers because they simply echo the beliefs of their audience. Echo chambers are dangerous, because they can be used to divide groups of people and set them against each other—without the audience even being aware that they are being manipulated through biased content. In a paper published in the journal *Scientific Reports* in 2024, researchers write:

> An echo chamber is a closed system where other voices are excluded by omission, causing your beliefs to become amplified or reinforced. In turn, these bubbles can boost social polarization and extreme political views, and, unfortunately, there is strong evidence that echo chambers exist in social media. . . . The crucial problem with echo chambers is that they deprive people (social media users) of a reality check, leaving them in a virtual reality.[29]

Alternative Social Media Platforms

During the COVID-19 pandemic and 2020 US elections, traditional social media platforms, including Facebook, X, and YouTube, began to crack down on misinformation. Not only did they flag certain posts as inaccurate, they also prevented them from being shared. They even banned some users for repeated violations of their community standards. As a result, many social media users migrated to alternative social media platforms, including BitChute, Gab, Gettr, Parler, Rumble, Telegram, and Truth Social, seeking greater freedom of speech.

According to a 2022 report by the Pew Research Center, 66 percent of those who regularly get news from at least one of the alternative social media sites identify as Republicans or lean toward the Republican Party. A significant portion of these users (15 percent) were banned from or prevented from earning money on the traditional social media platforms. Sixty-five percent of the users of alternative social media sites say that they have found a community of like-minded people on these platforms. Most of those who get news from the alternative sites—53 to 69 percent—describe the discussions on these sites as mostly friendly. Meanwhile, critics of the alternative platforms believe they serve as echo chambers for a conservative point of view, adding to the polarization of public discourse.

Echo chambers ensure that users not only see a limited set of opinions, they also see limited sets of facts. Data that contradicts their beliefs is downplayed or not given at all. As a result, some who refuse to consider contrary views adopt alternate sets of "facts"; they accept only what fits their views and dismiss even well-supported or proven evidence. People on both sides of the political divide acknowledge the situation. A 2020 survey by the Pew Research Center found that 80 percent of all US adults—regardless of their political affiliations—believe that people today not only disagree about governmental policies, they also disagree about the facts underlying those policies. The lack of consensus about what is true and what is false makes governance difficult. Because people do not agree on what is causing the problem, they cannot agree on the policies aimed at solving the problem.

Social Media Reinforces Bias

Social media is impacting how people get their news and information. And social media is often blamed for spreading misinformation easily and without consequences. According to a November 2023 survey by the Pew Research Center, about 50 percent of US adults go to social media apps for news. Nineteen percent of people turn to social media apps for news often, and 31 percent look there sometimes. Facebook, YouTube, Instagram, TikTok, and X are the main platforms people use for news. Much of the growth in news consumption came from TikTok. The number of TikTok users who regularly go to the site for news doubled from 2020 to 2023. The problem is not with the increased consumption of news and opinions in social media but rather with the sheer amount of information and misinformation that viewers are exposed to. Cognitive biases, for better or worse, help viewers sort through the deluge of texts, sounds, and images.

To increase user engagement, social media networks use algorithms to serve up news that caters to users' interests and therefore often to their biases. As a result, social media news might not present a diversity of viewpoints. It typically serves as an echo chamber for already-held beliefs. "As algorithms show users more of what they already like and engage with, users are less likely to encounter content that challenges their existing beliefs and biases," states a team of researchers at AIContentfy, a content creation platform. "This can lead to a highly polarized and fragmented political discourse, where people are less likely to engage with ideas that are different from their own."[30]

> "As algorithms show users more of what they already like and engage with, users are less likely to encounter content that challenges their existing beliefs and biases."[30]
>
> —Researchers at AIContentfy

Navigating a Sea of Bias

All opinions are biased, and even though many news sources try to remain factual in their reporting, it is still common for these sources to retain a slant, especially a political leaning to the left or right. Understanding those slants can help prepare readers or

According to a November 2023 survey by the Pew Research Center, about 50 percent of US adults turn to social media apps for news.

viewers for the way those sources present information. And while many long-standing newspapers, magazines, and websites have declared political leanings, for example, social media information sources may be short-lived or have no discernable pedigree. Therefore, audiences should be skeptical and seek to determine what might or might not make these sources reliable.

Experts at the University of Wisconsin–Green Bay say that it is important for internet users to evaluate information instead of simply consuming it. Users should ask themselves whether the information they are consuming seems fair and impartial. Is the information based on fact or on opinion? Users should watch for the use of extreme or inappropriate language. Such language is often a sign that the information is appealing to emotion rather than reason or is exhibiting bias toward specific groups. "Deliberately misleading news plays on your emotions, it can make you angry or happy or scared," states the university library's website. "Writers of 'fake' news know that articles that appeal to extreme emotion are more likely to get clicks. If an article makes you really angry or super sad, check those facts!"[31]

According to Sissel McCarthy, a writer for News Literacy Matters, when a writer or organization is advocating a point of view, bias is expected and can be considered. In such cases, the reader should consciously seek out an opposing viewpoint, just to see what the other side has to say. "It is incumbent on you, the news consumer, to seek out those facts and other points of view to come to your own, informed conclusions,"[32] says McCarthy. For example, a student who wants to do a report about the abortion debate should search online sites for groups with views on both sides of this issue. The groups on one side of a controversial issue cannot be expected to give credit to the arguments of the other side or even to include them. The student must proactively search out the two sides and evaluate the arguments to develop a well-informed, balanced report.

> "Deliberately misleading news plays on your emotions, it can make you angry or happy or scared. . . . If an article makes you really angry or super sad, check those facts!"[31]
>
> —University of Wisconsin–Green Bay

Aiming for a Balance of Opinions

McCarthy suggests that to avoid echo chambers, information consumers should take an inventory of the news sources they visit regularly. "A one-day, honest news audit can be quite revealing," says McCarthy. She suggests that internet users compare the list of news outlets they visit to the Media Bias Chart published by Ad Fontes Media, a US-based media watchdog and public benefit corporation. The chart, which is available online, measures the bias of a news source on the x-axis and its reliability on the y-axis. Left-leaning publications are placed on the left side of the x-axis, and right-leaning publications are on the right. The reliability of facts and claims within these publications is measured on the y-axis, with reliable publications appearing near the top of the axis and unreliable publications near the bottom. "If most of your news outlets fall to one side or near the bottom of the chart, consider adding some more reliable sources or viewpoints," says McCarthy. "Or check out the Associated Press and Reuters, two of the highest rated, most trustworthy and neutral news organizations at the top of the chart."[33]

McCarthy also suggests that news consumers visit the website AllSides, which offers coverage of current events from the left, right, and center of the political spectrum. The website presents three articles on each topic it covers. One article is labeled "From the Left," one is labeled "From the Center," and one is labeled "From the Right." For example, under the headline "20 Palestinians Killed While Waiting for Aid," the website presents a story

Using Self-Awareness to Counter Bias

Aliza Vigderman, a senior editor for Security.org, a website providing security product reviews, cautions readers not to trust their gut when they encounter online information. "When we like data and can process it easily, we're more likely to trust it," Vigderman writes. "However, this 'gut feeling' is very different from authentic expertise, so unless you're an expert on a subject, it's best not to trust your gut." Vigderman also cautions readers to watch out for three types of "mental blind spots":

Confirmation bias: Humans tend to look for information that conforms to their already-held beliefs, as it's easier to build neural pathways for information that we already know. Confirmation bias only increases when strong emotions are involved, as it makes it harder to break down these pathways with contradictory information.

Narrative fallacy: We're also more likely to fall for narratives rather than hard facts and figures, preferring stories with clear causes and effects over hard evidence. Narrative fallacy is often combined with confirmation bias, as we're especially likely to believe a story if it conforms to our preconceived notions.

Halo effect: Just because someone is attractive, funny, or confident, doesn't mean they're telling us the truth. But we're way more likely to believe them anyway.

Aliza Vigderman, "Misinformation and Disinformation: A Guide for Protecting Yourself," Security.org, February 21, 2024. www.security.org.

Depending on their political leanings, different publications may present the same news story in very different ways.

from CNN entitled "Attack Kills 20 and Injures 155 at Gaza Food Aid Point, as Israel Denies Responsibility" as a story from the left. Beside that article is one from the *Hill* entitled "Israel, Hamas Offer Competing Stories After at Least 20 Palestinians Die Waiting for Aid" offered as an account from the center. And beside that story is one from the *Washington Times* entitled "IDF [Israeli Defense Force] Says Hamas Behind Attack on Humanitarian Convoy That Killed Gazans Waiting for Aid"[34] as an example from the right. Although covering the same event, the three accounts—as their titles suggest—contrast sharply in assigning responsibility for the tragedy.

Lateral Reading

Seeking out news sources with alternative opinions or verifying the accuracy and biases of specific sources is often referred to as lateral reading. The term *lateral* refers to opening a series of tabs in a web browser to seek additional information about a news source, instead of reading "vertically," or only within that source. Readers might investigate how a news outlet is funded to reveal a potential bias in its reporting. For example, if the news source is funded by a political party, a corporation, or an advocacy group, it is likely to present news stories and opinions that cast the funding organization in a positive light. "Open a new tab and perform a web search to see what OTHER sources say about the reputation of your author and the publisher of the information," advises a handout on lateral reading from the University of Wisconsin– Green Bay. The handout also suggests that news consumers can look up the author, the news outlet, or even the specific news story to see if the fact-checking websites have already assessed the information. Many legitimate news outlets willingly announce their political leanings, and some sites, like AllSides and even Wikipedia, assess and clarify the biases of various news sources. Finally, the handout advises users to "check other sources to see if you can find significant contrasting claims. If you do, you may need to look at your source more closely."[35]

Conducting lateral reading can also provide opposing or alternate views related to resources that readers commonly consult. Experts suggest breaking out of echo chambers to read widely on subjects and become more receptive to differing opinions. Lateral reading is one way to find alternate views from a variety of sources.

Even when conducting lateral reading, media consumers must recognize that bias exists in nearly all news coverage. The fact that a news outlet or author has a bias is not necessarily bad. What is important is that these consumers become aware of biases—their own and those of their news outlets—to avoid being trapped in echo chambers that hamper them from acquiring a broader perspective on important issues.

Eluding Online Scammers

Misty Traska is a rabid Pittsburgh Steelers fan. Her dad and cousins are, too. As Christmas 2023 approached, Traska had a brainstorm for an unusual Christmas gift. The Steelers had made the playoffs and would be playing the Cincinnati Bengals at Acrisure Stadium in Pittsburgh on December 23. Traska decided to surprise her father with tickets to the big game. "I wanted to get him these tickets as a special Christmas present,"[36] she later told her local television news station in Pittsburgh. "Just a special moment between a daughter and a father, you know, getting to go to a game together, seeing the team that we love."[37] Her father, a Korean War veteran, had moved to Georgia and had not been to a Steelers game for fifteen years. Traska's cousins are also veterans, and she wanted to include them, too. "They're extra deserving of these tickets and this heartwarming experience,"[38] she says.

Traska looked for tickets on Ticketmaster, but she could not afford the prices. She turned to Facebook Marketplace and was delighted to find four tickets to the game for a total of five hundred dollars—a real bargain. She sent the money to the seller, located in Port St. Lucie, Florida, through the digital payments service Zelle. The payment was confirmed, but the tickets did not arrive. When Traska followed up, the seller said she was having issues sending the tickets electronically and that she would just send them via overnight mail. Traska soon received a Priority Mail envelope sent via the US Post Office, but there were no tickets inside. "When I got this envelope and this blank piece of paper, I automatically knew it was a scam and I got duped," says Traska. She searched for the seller's name online and learned that the woman had served time in a Florida jail. "I was angry, I was angry," Traska says. "This woman has done this before. She's had charges brought against her, a felony charge for selling Green Bay Packers tickets in 2016."[39]

Seeking Legitimate Sellers

With the high price of tickets, fans of moderate means are desperate to find bargains online. This makes them vulnerable to ticket sale scams. Such scams are especially common with sold-out events, such as Beyoncé's 2023 Renaissance World Tour, Taylor Swift's 2023–2024 Eras Tour, and sporting events such as the Super Bowl and the Olympics. The tickets are so sought after, and the fans are so devoted to their favorite stars, that people are willing to take risks with their money. Liz Ziegler, a fraud prevention director for Lloyds Bank, says:

> It's easy to let our emotions get the better of us when we find out our favorite artist is going to be performing live, but it's important not to let that excitement cloud our judgement when trying to get hold of tickets. Fraudsters are always changing their tactics to trick victims out of their hard-earned cash. With demand to attend live events soaring as the warmer weather approaches, they'll waste no time in targeting music fans as they rush to pick up tickets for the most popular gigs and festivals.[40]

To avoid scams, ticket buyers—and buyers of any product or service online—should confirm the legitimacy of the website before proceeding with a transaction. "Be careful and make sure you're booking through a legitimate site by checking the website address to make sure it is the official one," says Kirsty Adams, an

Bargain-hunting fans are vulnerable to ticket sale scams for high-priced and sold-out events, such as Beyoncé's 2023 Renaissance Tour.

online fraud expert at Barclays. "When you're caught up in the excitement and rush of trying to get a ticket, it can be really easy to stray from genuine ticket sites and not realize you're falling into the hands of a scammer."[41]

Amy Iverson, a technology reporter for the *Deseret News*, recommends that internet users type the address into the search bar directly, rather than clicking on links to website pages. "As in all cases of digital life, never click through to a website from emails, texts or online ads," says Iverson. "Even sponsored links can lead to copycat, fake webpages."[42]

According to the University of Wisconsin–Madison's cybersecurity website, if the website does business, its URL should have an "s" after "http," as in *https*. The "s" stands for

> "As in all cases of digital life, never click through to a website from emails, texts or online ads. Even sponsored links can lead to copycat, fake webpages."[42]
>
> —Amy Iverson, technology reporter for the *Deseret News*

How to Avoid Pharmacy Fraud

About 25 percent of internet shoppers have bought prescription medicines from online pharmacies. Buying online is convenient, private, and often far less expensive than buying from a local pharmacy. However, according to research conducted by the National Association of Boards of Pharmacy, 95 percent of online pharmacies do not follow the US Food and Drug Administration (FDA) guidelines for proper care. Many of these pharmacies are located outside the United States and are not governed by US laws and agencies. The medicines sold by these websites may have no active ingredients, may not be in the correct dosages, may be contaminated, or may be out of date. As a result, buyers can get sick instead of better, and they may experience dangerous side effects.

The FDA offers tips for buying from a legitimate pharmacy. It suggests doing business only with websites that require the user to provide a written prescription from a doctor (not just fill out an online form), list a physical address and telephone number in the United States, are licensed by the buyer's state, and offer the option to discuss a prescription with a licensed pharmacist.

"secure." It indicates that the site is using a Secure Sockets Layer Certificate. This lets the user know that all communication and data is encrypted as it passes from the user's browser to the website's server. The user should also see an icon in the search bar before the URL. In Bing this may appear as a padlock. In Chrome it may be a dot followed by a dash, with a dash followed by a dot below. Clicking these icons lets the user view security information about the site.

Iverson recommends buying tickets from the venue itself because it will be the most secure. However, many venues partner with authorized ticket brokers and third-party sellers. Iverson says buyers should check to make sure the ticket broker is on the venue's list of brokers. She explains:

> You can check to see if the broker is legit by asking the venue which sellers are authorized to sell for them or check to see if they're a member of the National Association of Ticket Brokers. The organization partners with the Better Business Bureau to ensure members have a customer protection policy. Also, simply search the name of the seller along with the word "scam" to see if any negative reviews pop up.[43]

The National Association of Ticket Brokers (NATB) lists more than 170 members, sortable by zip code, and offers a 200 percent guarantee, which states: "When you order a ticket from an NATB Member, they will deliver your tickets or will refund you 200% of the price of your tickets. In some cases, the NATB Member will not be able to provide the exact tickets you've ordered and will offer you comparable, or better tickets at the same or a lower price than you originally paid."[44]

Foiling the Fraudsters

Tickets are not the only hot commodity that people are looking for. Health and beauty aids, cryptocurrency, student financial aid, gaming accessories—the list of online products is virtually endless. Online scammers hawking these items are endless, too. But there are precautions that buyers can take to lessen the likelihood of falling victim to fraud.

Technology reporters Molly Greeves and Sarah Bridge recommend that consumers making purchases on the internet pay with a credit card, not with a bank card. "Bank transfers offer little protection if something goes wrong," Greeves and Bridge write. "Buyers who pay by credit card or debit card are better protected by . . . rules which say that you might be able to get your money back if something you paid for arrived broken or faulty, or didn't arrive at all." Services like PayPal and Venmo also offer protection when paying for goods and services, but users of these services should be careful in identifying the payment as going to a vendor of goods, not a friend. Or as Greeves and Bridge write, "If you do use PayPal, then select 'Paying for an item or service' from the payment options which will protect you under PayPal's Purchase Protection."[45] Any seller who insists on being given money through the "friends and family" transfer option is likely a scam artist. Similarly, buyers should never make payments with cash or gift cards. The FBI warns that such transactions are never guaranteed against theft or fraud.

The FBI reports that Americans lost more than $10.3 billion to online fraud in 2022. While teens and young adults are generally

Services like PayPal offer protection when paying for goods and services, although users should identify the payment as going to a vendor, not a friend.

more savvy than older adults about internet use, research shows that they are increasingly vulnerable to online fraud. A study by the online investigation service Social Catfish found that from 2017 to 2022, the largest percentage increase in money lost to scams was attributable to teens and children. Financial losses increased nearly 2,500 percent in this group over the five-year study period.

One reason that teens and young adults are vulnerable to online scams is that they can be overconfident in their internet use. They often lack life experiences that teach caution. They also may be impatient to gain wealth and other advantages. "They just rush into things," says a man named Chris, a former online scammer who works as a consultant for Social Catfish. "That's mainly the reason these young people get scammed."[46]

One popular scam involves cryptocurrency. These digital currencies have seen fantastic growth over short time

"They just rush into things. That's mainly the reason these young people get scammed."[46]

—Chris, a consultant for Social Catfish

42

periods. Young adults often see them as a fast and affordable way to gain financial status. "Most of them want quick money," explains Chris. "They want to invest in coin, they want to get more money, they want to double that money."[47] Buyers pay the seller but often receive nothing in return.

Phishing for Data

The goals of other internet users may be more mundane and have little to do with getting rich quickly. They may simply want more chances to win at an online game, more accessories for their video game characters, or a chance to win an online contest. Whatever the offer, the goal of the scammer is to obtain the user's bank or credit card information. This process is known as phishing. Phishers may offer a product, service, or even a free trial that can only be secured with credit card information. Once the phisher has the financial information, the transaction will end without the customer receiving anything. The phisher can use the financial information to take money from the account or purchase items that can be resold for cash.

Some phishers are not seeking financial information. They only want the internet user's personal information—phone number, email address, and mailing address. These personal details can be sold to companies that market products and services via text message and email. Some online scams offer links to sensational news stories, photos, or videos. To see the content, users are required to share their personal information—their email address, phone number, or even birth date. The phishing scam preys on basic human curiosity and the desire to know things that others do not know or see things that others have not seen. Users often feel that giving up information such as an email address or telephone number is a small price to pay to acquire information that lets them feel like they are smarter than their peers.

Sometimes scammers do not want any information. They only want a user to click a link or download a document. For example, an online ad might read, "Secret details about the raid on P. Diddy's mansions!" This type of scam plays on people's fascination with celebrity news. When the person clicks the link to see the story, they are taken to a page that tells them to download the latest edition of a popular software. Although the action may seem harmless, it can implant a computer virus, spyware, or ransomware into a user's device. Such a program, often called malware, then makes copies of itself, which it then sends to other computers. Some viruses damage data files on the devices they enter. Other malware, known as spyware, collects personal and sensitive information that it sends to advertisers, data collection firms, or malicious actors who can sell the information for a profit.

Ransomware is a program that can lock the user out of an electronic device until a sum of money is paid. There may be no telltale signs that the invitation to click such a link is dangerous. Experts suggest that internet users make it a rule never to act on information or offers that require them to click on a link.

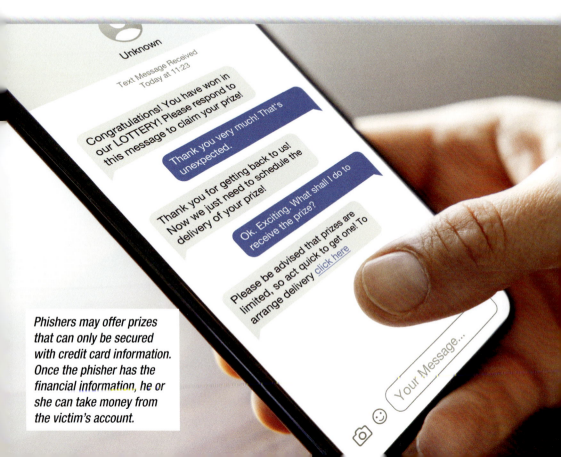

Phishers may offer prizes that can only be secured with credit card information. Once the phisher has the financial information, he or she can take money from the victim's account.

Slam the Scam

Every year, the Social Security Administration (SSA) sponsors a national Slam the Scam Day to raise awareness of government-related scams. The SSA coordinates with other US government agencies to publish posters, blogs, and social media posts warning of scams and how to avoid them. In January 2024 the SSA put out a scam alert with tips on avoiding online scams:

Recognize scammers. They may:

- **PRETEND** to be from an agency or organization you know.
- Say there's a **PROBLEM** or promise a prize.
- **PRESSURE** you to act immediately.
- Tell you to **PAY** in a specific way.

How to avoid a scam:

- **Remain calm.** Talk to someone you trust.
- **Hang up or ignore** the message. **DO NOT** click on links or attachments.
- **Protect your money.** Criminals will insist that you pay in a hard-to-trace manner, such as with a gift card, prepaid debit card, cryptocurrency, wire transfer, money transfer, or by mailing cash.
- **Protect your personal information.** Be skeptical of a contact you didn't initiate.
- **Spread the word.** Share your knowledge of Social Security–related scams. Post on social media using the hashtag #SlamtheScam to share your experience and warn others. . . . Please also share with your friends and family.

Social Security Administration, "Scam Alert," January 2024. www.ssa.gov.

Doing business online is commonplace. But internet users should not respond to offers that are sent to them via text, email, or even social media. They should only respond to offers that they seek out themselves. If they find a product or service through their own independent search, and it is sold by a reputable company that provides refunds when customers are dissatisfied, then it is likely to be genuine. Offers that cannot be verified should be shunned, no matter how enticing the offer may be.

CHAPTER FIVE

Avoiding Imposters

Michelle Singletary, a columnist for the *Washington Post*, received a phone call from a man who said he was contacting her on behalf of Publishers Clearing House, the well-known sweepstakes company. He told Singletary that she was the lucky winner of a $2.5 million award in the company's annual cash giveaways. Not only that, said the man, who identified himself as Frank Cooper, but she would also receive a champagne white S-Class Mercedes-Benz. Cooper gave Singletary the check number for her huge prize and had her repeat the number back to him. Cooper added that a licensed merchant banker in her area was ready to give her a locked briefcase with the check inside. He gave her the combination code so she could unlock the briefcase, and again he had her read the number back to him. It all sounded fine, but there was a slight bump in the road to riches. "But you can't get the money unless you register with the IRS [Internal Revenue Service] and pay a fee of $8,000,"[48] Cooper said.

Singletary was skeptical. "Wait, if this is a prize, why do I have to pay a fee?" she asked. Cooper raised his voice. "Ma'am, do you want your money or not? How do you not know that you must register with the IRS?" Cooper instructed Singletary to withdraw the cash from her back account, put it into two envelopes—each containing $4,000—and wrap the envelopes in newspaper. She should then proceed to the nearest FedEx Office and call Cooper back to get the address of where to overnight the package of cash. When Singletary asked what proof she would have that Cooper had received the cash, he told her to "get insurance on the mailing." Sensing that Singletary was becoming skeptical, Cooper put his general manager, someone named Ray Kingston, on the line. "Are you ready to send the money?" Kingston asked. Singletary was not. "Now, you know this is a scam,"[49] she said. The caller said nothing. The next thing Singletary heard was a dial tone.

An Army of Imposters

Singletary's experience is not unique. Many people receive calls from people offering phony gifts. Other impersonators say they are calling from the IRS. According to the Treasury Inspector General for Tax Administration (TIGTA), during October 2013 to March 2022, more than 2.5 million taxpayers reported that they had been contacted by individuals who claimed to be IRS employees. Typically, the imposters would tell the victims that they owed additional taxes and that if they did not immediately pay, they would be arrested or face other adverse consequences. According to TIGTA, 16,038 people believed the scammers and sent them money. The losses stemming from IRS impersonation cases during the period amount to $85 million. Experts believe the numbers are likely much higher, because people do not always report the scams to authorities.

Christopher Brown, an attorney at the Federal Trade Commission, advises users to ignore phone calls and even emails that purport to be from the IRS. "If the IRS contacts you, they're never going to contact you first via email or telephone—they're going to contact you in writing a letter," says Brown. He adds that an IRS agent will not demand immediate payment or threaten users with arrest. "That's a sure sign that it's a scam,"[50] Brown says. On its

> "If the IRS contacts you, they're never going to contact you first via email or telephone—they're going to contact you in writing a letter."[50]
>
> —Christopher Brown, an attorney at the Federal Trade Commission

Late night calls from unknown callers are a red flag. Reputable organizations, such as the Internal Revenue Service, will never contact consumers in this manner.

website, the IRS states that generally it will first mail a bill to any taxpayer who owes taxes and that it will never demand immediate payment, threaten immediate arrest, fail to give citizens a chance to dispute any tax debt, or call about a tax refund. The IRS advises that taxpayers who receive harassing phone calls should record the number, hang up, and report the call by calling or visiting the website of TIGTA and reporting the potential fraud.

Catfishing

Not all impersonators are out for money. Some are seeking attention and affection. Feeling unattractive and undeserving, they often pretend to be someone more attractive than they are. Typically, they use pictures of others as their own profile pictures in social media apps. They find the attention they receive from their victims to be gratifying. By assuming a fictional persona, they can say things they never would in real life. They enjoy the life of their alter ego. These people are known as catfishers, and the practice of creating a fictional persona to lure another person into an online relationship is known as catfishing.

Victims of catfishers do not know who is hiding behind the fictional persona. They believe that the alter ego is genuine and acting sincerely. And catfishers may be hiding more than their physical appearance. For example, it is common for much older people to pose as teens and young adults to see whether they can get young people to share intimate talk and photos with them. Catfishers may pose as a different gender to lure victims. According to the website FreeBackgroundChecks.com, around 24 percent of all catfishing perpetrators pose as a different gender.

Unfortunately, the victims of catfishers are often hurt by their fake friends. At first, the victims can be flattered and even excited to be chatting with an attractive stranger. Gradually, though, victims can form emotional bonds with their chat mates. They may be enticed to share intimate photos of themselves to gain the approval and affection of their online friends. Learning the truth about who the catfisher really is can be devastating. Catfishing victims can experience heartbreak, loss, or shame when they learn that they have been deceived. The shame is often worse if the victims have shared compromising photos or videos of themselves with the catfisher.

Romance Scams

Most catfishers are only seeking emotional rewards from their online relationships. Others, however, hope to reap financial gains. They often relate money problems that are taking time away from the online relationship, or they might request that the victim help pay for a plane ticket so that the two can meet. Many victims are eager to help those they believe love them. The Federal Trade Commission reports that there were more than sixty-four thousand reported cases of online romance scams in 2023. These scams resulted in losses of more than $1.1 billion in gifts and cash. "Con artists are adept at building a relationship of trust," explains Katie Hass, director of Utah's Division of Consumer Protection. "They prey on people who are genuinely seeking love, making them vulnerable to exploitation."[51]

If victims of a romance scam become wary of the requests their online lovers are making, the situation can take a dangerous turn. If a person being scammed has shared compromising photos, the catfisher will sometimes turn to extortion. He or she will threaten to show the photos to the victim's family and friends if his or her demands are not met.

Catfishers succeed in finding victims in part because so many relationships start online. A study by Michael Rosenfeld and Sonia Hausen of Stanford University and Reuben Thomas of the University of New Mexico found that the number of heterosexual couples who met online had doubled from about 20 percent in

> "Con artists are adept at building a relationship of trust. They prey on people who are genuinely seeking love, making them vulnerable to exploitation."[51]
>
> —Katie Hass, director of Utah's Division of Consumer Protection

Parent Sues Meta over Failure to Prevent Sextortion

Around midnight on July 27, 2022, recent high school graduate Gavin Guffey received an Instagram message from what appeared to be a young woman. After sharing nude pictures of herself, Gavin's new Instagram acquaintance asked him for a nude selfie. Gavin complied. Immediately, the person at the other end began to demand money and threatened to send Gavin's nude photo to his friends and family. Gavin sent the sextortionist twenty-five dollars from his Venmo account, but it was not enough. The sextortionist kept up the pressure. Believing he had no way to escape the humiliation, Gavin took his own life, just an hour and a half after the ordeal began. In January 2024 Gavin's father, Brandon Guffey, filed a wrongful death lawsuit against Meta, the parent company of Instagram. Guffey alleges that Meta does not have tools in place to protect underage users from catfishing, sextortion, and other online abuse. "Meta never does enough. It's ridiculous that these predators continue to come online and go after our children," says Brandon Guffey. "If I have a party on my property, and I invite everybody on there, I'm responsible for what happens on my property. And for some reason, we treat these digital companies different."

Quoted in Faith Karimi, "A South Carolina Lawmaker Is Suing Instagram After His Son Died by Suicide," CNN, January 30, 2024. www.cnn.com.

Catfishing victims initially think they have made an online friend. They can experience heartbreak, loss, or shame when they learn that they have been deceived.

2010 to nearly 40 percent by 2019. An even higher percentage of same-sex couples met online. About 65 percent of same-sex couples met online in 2010, and the number remained the same in 2019. Since meeting online is commonplace, single people are more open to both genuine relationship seekers and catfishers.

Catching a Catfisher

To avoid being victimized by a catfisher, people starting a relationship online should seek some kind of verification of the other person's identity as soon as possible. A simple first step is to hold a video chat. Seeing the person on-screen can confirm the other person's age, gender, and general appearance. "Make sure you know who you're talking to," says Chris, a consultant with Social Catfish, a company that verifies online identities for a fee. "You can see me in a video call right now. I can see you. I know you are you. If you're talking to someone who's not going to show you his face on a video call, it's an absolute scam."[52] An online acquaintance who always refuses to have a video call on short notice should not be trusted. Repeated delays give imposters time to find other people to appear on camera. For example, an older person might arrange for a younger person to appear in the video call to quell the fears of the person being catfished.

Video chats can be faked by having a friend or relative appear on-screen or even by using a deepfake program that projects a simulated face over the chatter's real image. Meeting in person is one sure way to verify that the person at least appears the same as in their profile. Catfishers usually avoid meeting in person. Social Catfish says that catfishers often claim they cannot meet because they are serving in the military or live overseas. The company recommends that people avoid chatting with others who make those claims. The FBI agrees. "Beware if the individual promises to meet in person but then always comes up with an

Meeting in person is one sure way to verify that a contact from an online dating site at least appears the same as in his or her profile.

A Million-Dollar Romance Scam

It is not only the young who can fall victim to a catfisher. The desire to find love can lead even experienced adults to give their hearts to online pretenders. This is what happened to Liza Likins, a former backup singer. She joined Facebook Dating and met a man with the profile name Donald. They started chatting, and things seemed to click. "I spoke with this man every day on the phone for maybe 4 or 5 hours a day," Likins said. "We became very, very close." As Donald got to know Likins better, he began to ask for money. Loyal and generous, Likins sent him money from her savings account. When Donald said he was falsely arrested and needed money for bail, Likins sold her house and sent him the proceeds. In all, Likins gave Donald more than $1 million. He said he would come to the United States to be with her, but it never happened. When Likins realized it was all a scam, she was devastated. "I think I just left my body and went into complete traumatic shock," she says. "I mean, I was speechless. I couldn't, I didn't know what to think or say."

Quoted in Anna Werner, "She Fell for a Romance Scam on Facebook. The Man Whose Photo Was Used Says It's Happened Before," CBS News, February 15, 2024. www.cbsnews.com.

excuse for why he or she can't," states the FBI. "If you haven't met the person after a few months, for whatever reason, you have good reason to be suspicious."[53]

The FBI suggests several simple steps a person can take to protect against catfishing. For example, the romance seeker should proceed slowly and ask the other person a lot of questions. He or she should watch for evasiveness and contradictions. An honest person's answers will be straightforward and consistent.

Anyone who has made a new acquaintance can use a search engine to see whether that person's name appears on social media websites such as Facebook and LinkedIn. If so, the information on those websites should be scrutinized to verify what the person has said in online chats.

> "Beware if the individual promises to meet in person but then always comes up with an excuse for why he or she can't. If you haven't met the person after a few months, for whatever reason, you have good reason to be suspicious."[53]
>
> —Federal Bureau of Investigation

Search engines can also turn up public profiles or news stories about an individual in question. Some fee-based websites allow users to conduct a search using an image. This can reveal whether a person's photos are associated with different names on other websites, suggesting that the photo is not really of the person doing the chatting.

The FBI advises that users should beware if a new contact suggests leaving the dating service or social media site to communicate directly via WhatsApp or another private chatting platform. Another red flag is if the individual attempts to isolate you from friends and family, suggesting that the relationship be kept secret. A definite warning sign is when an online acquaintance requests inappropriate photos or financial information that could later be used for extortion. The FBI strongly advises against sending money for any reason: "NEVER send money, cryptocurrency, or gift cards to anyone you have only communicated with online or by phone, regardless of how in love you are or how in love they say they are with you."[54]

Through email, text messaging, and video chats, the internet enables friends and family to stay in touch with each other as never before. At the same time, the internet offers a cloak of invisibility to strangers who seek to contact others for nefarious purposes. Internet users are so used to communicating online that they sometimes forget that there are predators online, doing nothing but searching for their next victim. To avoid being the victim of an online imposter, internet users need to always remain vigilant and demand proof that the people contacting them are who they say they are.

SOURCE NOTES

Introduction: Unfiltered Information

1. Quoted in Albawaba.com, "Did Israel Drop Cans Containing Explosives in Gaza?," January 23, 2024. www.msn.com.
2. Quds News Network (@QudsNen), "'According to local sources, Israeli jets dropped cans containing explosives as bait for starving displaced Palestinians in Al Mawasi in Southern Gaza,'" X, January 23, 2024. https://twitter.com/QudsNen/status/1749715184858358160.
3. Ryan McBeth, "Is Israel Dropping Booby Trapped Cans of Meat onto Gaza?," Official Ryan McBeth Substack, January 23, 2024. https://ryanmcbeth.substack.com.
4. Quoted in Richard Gray, "Lies, Propaganda and Fake News: A Challenge for Our Age," BBC, March 1, 2017. www.bbc.com.
5. Michael Adam with Clotilde Hocquard, "Artificial Intelligence, Democracy and Elections," European Parliamentary Research Service, 2023. www.europarl.europa.eu.

Chapter One: Identifying False and Misleading Information

6. Quoted in Stephen Orbanek, "Study Shows Verified Users Are Among Biggest Culprits When It Comes to Sharing Fake News," Temple Now, November 9, 2021. https://news.temple.edu.
7. New York Times Co. v. Sullivan, 376 U.S. 254 (1964).
8. Quoted in University of Birmingham, "'Fake News' Poses Corrosive Existential Threat to Democracy," July 27, 2022. www.birmingham.ac.uk.
9. Quoted in James Vincent, "YouTube Brings Back More Human Moderators After AI Systems Over-Censor," The Verge, September 21, 2020. www.theverge.com.
10. State of Missouri, et al. versus Joseph R. Biden Jr., et al., case no. 3:22-CV-01213 (2023).
11. Bantam Books, Inc. v. Sullivan, 372 U.S. 58 (1963).
12. Quoted in Shannon Bond and Natalie Escobar, "Appeals Court Slaps Biden Administration for Contact with Social Media Companies," NPR, September 8, 2023. www.npr.org.
13. Murthy v. Missouri, No. 23-411, March 18, 2024.

14. Quoted in Janna Anderson and Lee Rainie, "The Future of Truth and Misinformation Online," Pew Research Center, October 19, 2017. www.pewresearch.org.
15. National Center for State Courts, "Disinformation and the Public," July 27, 2022. www.ncsc.org.
16. Lindsay Boezi, "Fake News: How to Be a Responsible Information Consumer," MacPhaidin Library, January 26, 2022. https://libguides.stonehill.edu.
17. Quoted in Emily Gersema, "How Americans Can Help Stop Fake News," USC Today, December 1, 2020. https://today.usc.edu.
18. Fraser Hall Library, "Find Elections and Politics Information: Ways to Avoid the Spread of False Info on Social Media," December 20, 2023. https://library.geneseo.edu.

Chapter Two: Spotting Deepfakes and Altered Images

19. Quoted in Joseph Foley and Abi Le Guilcher, "22 of the Best Deepfake Examples That Terrified and Amused the Internet," Creative Bloq, January 15, 2024. www.creativebloq.com.
20. Quoted in *60 Minutes*, *How Synthetic Media, or Deepfakes, Could Soon Change Our World*, YouTube, October 10, 2021. https://youtube.com/Yb1GCjmw8_8?si=3tlX3_rymSnyXt6W.
21. Quoted in *60 Minutes*, *How Synthetic Media, or Deepfakes, Could Soon Change Our World*.
22. Quoted in Jane Wakefield, "Deepfake Presidents Used in Russia-Ukraine War," BBC, March 17, 2022. www.bbc.com.
23. Quoted in US Government Publishing Office, "Open Hearing: Worldwide Threat Assessment of the U.S. Intelligence Community," January 29, 2019. www.govinfo.gov.
24. Quoted in US Government Publishing Office, "Open Hearing."
25. Quoted in Intel News, "Intel Introduces Real-Time Deepfake Detector," November 14, 2022. www.intel.com.
26. Quoted in US Special Committee on Aging, "Casey Holds Hearing on Role of Artificial Intelligence in Frauds and Scams," November 16, 2023. www.aging.senate.gov.
27. Quoted in Jamie Joseph, "Scams Targeting Older Americans, Many Using AI, Caused over $1 Billion in Losses in 2022," Fox News, November 19, 2023. www.foxnews.com.
28. Quoted in Joseph, "Scams Targeting Older Americans, Many Using AI, Caused over $1 Billion in Losses in 2022."

Chapter Three: Recognizing Bias

29. Chen Avin et al., "On the Impossibility of Breaking the Echo Chamber Effect in Social Media Using Regulation," *Scientific Reports*, January 11, 2024. www.nature.com.
30. AIContentfy team, "The Impact of Social Media Algorithms on Content Distribution," AIContentfy, February 27, 2024. https://aicontentfy.com.
31. University of Wisconsin–Green Bay, "Identifying False & Misleading News," December 22, 2023. https://libguides.uwgb.edu.
32. Sissel McCarthy, "The Growing Threat of News Silos," News Literacy Matters, September 6, 2022. https://newsliteracymatters.com.
33. McCarthy, "The Growing Threat of News Silos."
34. Quoted in AllSides, "Balanced News from the Left, Center and Right," March 17, 2024. www.allsides.com.
35. University of Wisconsin–Green Bay, "Evaluating Sources Using Lateral Reading," January 16, 2024. https://libguides.uwgb.edu.

Chapter Four: Eluding Online Scammers

36. Quoted in Amy Hudak, "Woman Who Bought Steelers Tickets for Veterans in Her Family Scammed out of Money," Yahoo! News, December 11, 2023. https://news.yahoo.com.
37. Quoted in Lauren Linder, "Family of Veteran Allegedly Scammed out of Steelers Tickets," CBS News, December 10, 2023. www.cbsnews.com.
38. Quoted in Hudak, "Woman Who Bought Steelers Tickets for Veterans in Her Family Scammed out of Money."
39. Quoted in Hudak, "Woman Who Bought Steelers Tickets for Veterans in Her Family Scammed out of Money."
40. Quoted in Molly Greeves and Sarah Bridge, "Ticket Scams to Watch Out for This Year and How to Avoid Them," *Good Housekeeping*, January 16, 2024. www.goodhousekeeping.com.
41. Quoted in Greeves and Bridge, "Ticket Scams to Watch Out for This Year and How to Avoid Them."
42. Amy Iverson, "Buying Tickets for a Sold-Out Concert? Here's How to Make Sure Your Tickets Are the Real Deal," *Salt Lake City (NV) Deseret News*, July 17, 2023. www.deseret.com.
43. Iverson, "Buying Tickets for a Sold-Out Concert?"
44. National Association of Ticket Brokers, "Why NATB." www.natb.org.

45. Greeves and Bridge, "Ticket Scams to Watch Out for This Year and How to Avoid Them."
46. Quoted in Lisa Fletcher, "US Sees Alarming Surge in Online Scams Targeting Kids and Teens, Study Shows," ABC-7 News, October 2, 2023. https://wjla.com.
47. Quoted in Fletcher, "US Sees Alarming Surge in Online Scams Targeting Kids and Teens, Study Shows."

Chapter Five: Avoiding Imposters

48. Quoted in Michelle Singletary, "No, That Is Not the IRS Calling You," *Washington Post*, March 31, 2023. www.washingtonpost.com.
49. Quoted in Singletary, "No, That Is Not the IRS Calling You."
50. Quoted in Kaitlyn Radde, "No, the IRS Isn't Calling You. It Isn't Texting or Emailing You, Either," NPR, April 7, 2023. www.npr.org.
51. Quoted in Cristina Flores, "FTC Warns of $1.1 Billion Loss Due to Romance Scams in 2023," KJZZ 14, February 14, 2024. https://kjzz.com.
52. Quoted in Fletcher, "US Sees Alarming Surge in Online Scams Targeting Kids and Teens, Study Shows."
53. Federal Bureau of Investigation, "Romance Scams," March 25, 2020. www.fbi.gov.
54. Federal Bureau of Investigation, "Romance Scams."

FOR FURTHER RESEARCH

Books

Ben Boyington et al., *The Media and Me: A Guide to Critical Media Literacy for Young People*. New York: Triangle Square, 2022.

Becky Holmes, *Keanu Reeves Is Not in Love with You: The Murky World of Online Romance*. London: Unbound, 2024.

Stuart A. Kallen, *Spotting Online Scams and Fraud*. San Diego, CA: ReferencePoint, 2023.

Mark Last et al., eds., *Detecting Online Propaganda and Misinformation*. Singapore: World Scientific, 2024.

Carla Mooney, *Exploring Solutions: Online Disinformation and Misinformation*. San Diego, CA: ReferencePoint, 2023.

Don Nardo, *Misinformation: What It Is and How to Identify It*. San Diego, CA: ReferencePoint, 2023.

Internet Sources

Michael Adam with Clotilde Hocquard, "Artificial Intelligence, Democracy and Elections," European Parliamentary Research Service, 2023. www.europarl.europa.eu.

Federal Bureau of Investigation, "Romance Scams," March 25, 2020. www.fbi.gov.

Joseph Foley and Abi Le Guilcher, "22 of the Best Deepfake Examples That Terrified and Amused the Internet," Creative Bloq, January 15, 2024. www.creativebloq.com.

Intel, "Intel Introduces Real-Time Deepfake Detector," November 14, 2022. www.intel.com.

Pew Research Center, "Social Media and News Fact Sheet," November 15, 2023. www.pewresearch.org.

Galen Stocking et al., "The Role of Alternative Social Media in the News and Information Environment," Pew Research Center, October 6, 2022. www.pewresearch.org.

University of Wisconsin–Green Bay, "Identifying False & Misleading News," December 22, 2023. https://libguides.uwgb.edu.

Websites

AllSides
www.allsides.com
AllSides is a news website that provides readers with information and ideas from across the political spectrum. Under each news topic, the website presents three news stories—one labeled "From the Left," one labeled "From the Center," and one labeled "From the Right." Readers are encouraged to compare these stories to interpret information for themselves.

AP Fact Check
https://apnews.com/ap-fact-check
Part of the Associated Press, a news organization founded in 1846, AP Fact Check investigates dubious news stories from around the world. The website features a series called "Not Real News: A look at what didn't happen this week."

FactCheck.org
www.factcheck.org
FactCheck.org is a nonprofit website with the self-described mission of reducing the level of deception and confusion in US politics. The website features a "Viral Spiral" section devoted to debunking social media misinformation.

Pew Research Center: Internet & Technology
www.pewinternet.org
Through its Internet & Technology website, the Pew Research Center studies how Americans use the internet and how digital technologies are shaping the world today. Its website has the results of numerous studies about social media and the internet.

PolitiFact
www.politifact.com
Created by the *Tampa Bay Times* in 2007, PolitiFact is a nonpartisan fact-checking website dedicated to uncovering the truth in American politics. The organization's Truth-o-Meter icon labels statements as true, mostly true, half true, mostly false, false, and pants on fire.

Snopes
www.snopes.com
This fact-checking website has an easily searchable database that allows users to see what the Snopes investigators have learned about various social media posts and other online stories. Its fact-check articles often include links to documenting sources so readers can do independent research and make up their own minds.

INDEX

Note: Boldface page numbers indicate illustrations.

Adams, Kirsty, 38–39
Ad Fontes Media, 33–34
advertising, deepfakes in, 20
Afghanistan, 8
AIContentfy, 31
Alito, Samuel, 15–16
AllSides (website), 34, 36
anchoring bias, 28, 29
artificial intelligence (AI)
    deepfakes and
        creation of, 18–19, 23
        tools to detect, 22
    generative adversarial networks and, 23
    as tool to detect misinformation, 6–7, 12–13
Associated Press, 34
audio deepfakes, 22–24, **25**, 25–26

bad actors, intent of, 5
Bantam Books, Inc. v. Sullivan (1963), 14–15
Beyoncé's Renaissance Tour, 38, **39**
bias(es). *See* cognitive bias(es)
Biden, Joe, **28**
Bing, 26, 40
Boezi, Lindsay, 17
bots, 10
Brennan, William, 9, 14
Bridge, Sarah, 41
Brown, Christopher, 47–48

Casey, Bob, Jr., 23
catfishers/catfishing
    compromising photos and, 50
    described, 48–49
    financial losses from, 49–50
    sextortion, 50
    steps to protect against, 51–54
    warning signs of, 54
Ceylan, Gizem, 16
China, deepfake videos by, 20
Chrome, 26, 40
CNN, 35
Coats, Daniel R., 22
cognitive bias(es)
    as coping mechanism, 27
    dangers of, 29–30
    echo chambers and, 29–30
    mental blind spots and, 34
    social media reinforces, 30–31
    types of, 27–29, 34

computer viruses, 44
confirmation bias, 28–29, 34
consensus, 5–6
contest scams, 46–47
critical-thinking skills, 17
cryptocurrency, 42–43
Cybersecurity & Infrastructure Security Agency, 25

deepfakes
    in advertising, 20
    audio, 22–24, 25, 25–26
    cautionary messages about, 24
    creation of, 18–19, 23
    detection of, 22, 25–26
    Ford in Indiana Jones and the Dial of Destiny, 19
    future threats, 21–22
    generative adversarial networks and, 23
    number posted online (2023), 19
    scams and, 22–23
    of Swift, 18
    video, 19–22, 21
Deepfakes: The Coming Infocalypse (Schick), 20
deep learning technology, 18–19, 22
Deep Text, 12
de Jong, Bob, 24
democracy
    information's role in, 6
    lack of consensus about truthfulness of facts, 30
    spread of political misinformation and, 10–11
Doughty, Terry, 14–15

echo chambers, 29–30, 31
Edwards, Paul N., 16–17
Ekin, Tahir, 24, 25
event ticket scams, 37–38, **39**

Facebook
    catfishing on, 53
    Deep Text, 12
    Marketplace, 37–38
    as news source, 31
    sharers of misinformation on, 16
Facebook Dating, 53
fact-checking organizations, and detection of deepfakes, 26
fact-checking websites, **10**, 11–12
FactCheck.org, 11, 12
FakeCatcher, 22

fake news and democracy, 10–11
false speech, penalties for posting, 9
Federal Bureau of Investigation (FBI)
    amount lost to scams (2022), 41
    on Russian and Chinese deepfake videos, 20
    steps to protect against catfishing, 52–53, 54
Federal Trade Commission, 22, 49
Ferrara, Emilio, 17
Fifth Circuit Court of Appeals, 14–15
First Amendment and targeting misinformation,
    13–16
Ford, Harrison, 19
fraud. See scams
FreeBackgroundChecks.com, 49
freedom of speech, targeting misinformation
    and suppressing, 13–16
Freeman, Morgan, 24
Frontiers in Psychology (journal), 13

generative adversarial networks, 23
gifts as scams, 46–47
Google, 12–13, 26
Greeves, Molly, 41
Guffey, Brandon, 50
Guffey, Gavin, 50

halo effect, 34
Hass, Katie, 49–50
Hausen, Sonia, 50–51
Hill (newspaper), 35
Holtzapple, LeAnn, 23–24
Holtzapple, Terry, 23–24

Indiana Jones and the Dial of Destiny (movie),
    19
information, role of, in democracy, 6
Instagram
    Deep Text, 12
    example of sextortion on, 50
    as news source, 31
Iverson, Amy, 39, 40

lateral reading, 35–36
Lewandowsky, Stephan, 6
Likins, Liza, 53
Louisiana, 14, 15–16

malware, 44
Masaryk, Radomír, 13
McBeth, Ryan, 4
McCarthy, Sissel, 33, 34
Media Bias Chart, 33–34
mental blind spots, 34
Meta
    failure to prevent sextortion by, 50
    identification of false news and
        misinformation and, 11, 13
Mikkelson, Barbara, 11
Mikkelson, David, 11

misinformation
    democracy and spread of political, 10–11
    described, 4
    detection of, 6–7, 11, 12–13
    First Amendment and, 13–16
    percentage of Americans encountering, on
        social media, 8
    reasons for posting, 9–11
    social media and spread of, 5, 6
        by Americans, 8–9
        habitual sharers, 16
        penalties for, 9
        policing, 12–13
        using critical-thinking skills and, 17
Missouri, 14, 15–16
Mohan, Neal, 13
Murthy v. Missouri (2024), 15–16

narrative fallacies, 34
National Association of Boards of Pharmacy, 40
National Association of Ticket Brokers (NATB),
    40, 41
National Center for State Courts, 17
news sources
    evaluating information, 32–33
    inventory of, 33–34
    seeking opposing viewpoints, 34–36, 35
    social media as, 31, 32, 32–33
New York Times Co. v. Sullivan (1964), 9

Oh, Genevieve, 19
Olympics, 38
online dating sites, **52**, 53, 54
online pharmacies, 40
online purchases, paying for, 41, **42**

Pang, Min-Seok, 9
PayPal, 41, **42**
Pew Research Center, 30, 31, **32**
pharmacy scams, 40
phishers/phishing, 43, **44**
political misinformation, 9–11
PolitiFact, 11
prescription medicine scams, 40
*Proceedings of the National Academy of
    Sciences*, 16
propaganda and deepfake videos, 20–21, **21**
public opinion, on truthfulness of facts, 30

Quds News Network, 4

ransomware, 44
Reglitz, Merten, 10–11
Reuters, 34
reverse image searches, 26
Reyes, Carlos, 8
Rhode Island, 14–15
Riparbelli, Victor, 20
romance scams, 49–50, 53

Rosenfeld, Michael, 50–51
Russia, deepfake videos by, 20–21, **21**

Sardarizadeh, Shayan, 21
Sasse, Ben, 22
scams
  amount lost (2022) to, 41
  avoiding, 38–41, 45
  catfishing
    compromising photos and, 50
    described, 48–49
    financial losses from, 49–50
    sextortion, 50
    steps to protect against, 51–54
    warning signs of, 54
  contest winnings as, 46–47
  cryptocurrency, 42–43
  gifts as, 46–47
  IRS impersonators calling or emailing for
    owed taxes, 47–48
  malware implanted in user's computer and,
    44
  payment methods for online purchases and,
    41, 42
  pharmacy, 40
  phishing and, 43, 44
  romance, 49–50
  teenagers and children as victims of, 41–42
  ticket sales, 37–38
  See also deepfakes
Schick, Nina, 20
Schouwink, Boet, 24
Scientific Reports (journal), 29
Secure Sockets Layer Certificates, 40
Security.org, 34
sextortion, 50
Singletary, Michelle, 46–47
Slam the Scam Day, 45
Snoop Dogg, 20
Snopes, **10**, 11
Social Catfish, 42, 52
social media
  AI used to detect misinformation on, 6–7,
    12–13
  alternative platforms, 30
  biases as reinforced by, 30–31
  as echo chamber, 31
  as news source, 31, 32, 32–33
  percentage of Americans encountering
    misinformation on, 8
  romantic relationships beginning on, 49–51,
    52, 53, 54
  spread of deepfake videos on, 21
  spread of misinformation on, 5, 6
    by Americans, 8–9
    bots, 10
    identifying, 11
    policing, 6–7, 12–13
  using critical-thinking skills before sharing, 17

Social Security Administration (SSA), 45
software filters, focus of, 5
Splendid Savage Podcast, The (Reyes), 8
spyware, 44
Statista, 8–9, 12–13
Super Bowl games, 38
Swift, Taylor, 18, **19**, 38
Synthesia, 20
synthetic media. *See* deepfakes
synthetic reality, 24

teenagers
  ability of, to detect misinformation, 13
  catfishers posing as, 49
  as victims of scams, 41–42
ThisPersonDoesNotExist.com (website), 23
Thomas, Reuben, 50–51
TikTok, as news source, 31
Traska, Misty, 37–38
Treasury Inspector General for Tax
  Administration (TIGTA), 47

Ukraine, 8, 20–21
Unapologetic Patriot Mama, 8, 9
unconscious bias, 27
University of Southern California, 16
University of Wisconsin–Green Bay, 32, 36
University of Wisconsin–Madison, 39–40
Urban Legends Reference Pages, **10**, 11
US Constitution and targeting misinformation,
  13–16
US Food and Drug Administration (FDA)
  guidelines, 40
US Internal Revenue Service (IRS), 47–48
US Supreme Court, free speech decisions,
  14–16

Venmo, 41
videos
  catfishers and, 51–52
  deepfake
    cautionary messages about, 24
    creating, 18–19
    detecting, 22, 25, 26
    examples of, 19–21, 21
    future threat of, 21–22
    removed from YouTube, 12–13
Vigderman, Aliza, 34

Washington Times (newspaper), 35
Wikipedia, 36

X (social media platform), as news source, 31

Yale University, 16
YouTube, 12–13, 31

Zelenskyy, Volodymyr, 21, **21**
Ziegler, Liz, 38

PICTURE CREDITS

Cover: SeventyFour/Shutterstock

6: Ground Picture/Shutterstock

10: Michael Vi/Alamy Stock Photo

15: Jeff Bukowski/Shutterstock

19: Martha Asencio-Rhine/ZUMAPRESS/Newscom

21: Yanosh Nemesh/Shutterstock

25: fizkes/Shutterstock

28: CJ Hanevy/Shutterstock

32: fizkes/Shutterstock

35: Richard Levine/Alamy Stock Photo

39: PatBo/EGA/Newscom/SLMIA/Newscom

42: Chonlachai/Shutterstock

44: Kaspars Grinvalds/Shutterstock

48: Tero Vesalainen/Shutterstock

51: shurkin_son/Shutterstock

52: Dragon Images/Shutterstock

ABOUT THE AUTHOR

Bradley Steffens is a novelist, poet, and award-winning author of more than seventy nonfiction books for children and young adults.